Text copyright © 2013 by Mike Dooley

Text previously published by Atria Books/Beyond Words Publishing in *Choose Them Wisely* © 2009

Jacket art, interior illustrations, and book design © 2013 by Virginia Allyn http://www.virginiaallyn.com

You are adored.

Published by Totally Unique Thoughts®
A division of TUT® Enterprises, Inc.
Orlando, Florida - http://www.tut.com
Manufactured in China.

10 9 8 7 6 5 4 3 2
ISBN: 978-0-9814602-7-7

Dreams Come True
All They Need Is You!

WRITTEN BY
Mike Dooley

ILLUSTRATED BY
Virginia Allyn

TUT
DOT
COM

The world is your oyster
And life is your ocean,
Just follow your dreams
To set the waves in motion.

A celebration of stars
Dance into the night,
One for each dream
About to take flight.
And by dawn's early hour
They all have a plan,
To burst into your life
As fast as they can.
But you've got to believe
That dreams really come true,
If you want all the gifts
That are waiting for you!

I've started a journey
I'll see through to the end,
And I'm ever so grateful
It includes you,
My friend.

Over the moon
And past the stars,
When you dream with a friend
You fly twice as far.

Far out in the ocean
On a moonlit night,
A circle of dolphins
Slips out of sight.
They're on a mission
Of the grandest scale.
To spread the word
To every minnow and whale:
That life's an illusion
Just waiting for you,
To believe in your dreams
So that they can come true.

The deep blue sea
Spoke to me,
It was holding back
A mystery.
A dolphin took me by the hand,
It wanted me to understand:
That in this life
There's more to behold,
Than bags of money and pots of gold.
Believe in yourself
And you will see,
How happy and free
You were meant to be.

It's the little things you do,
That make the big things happen.

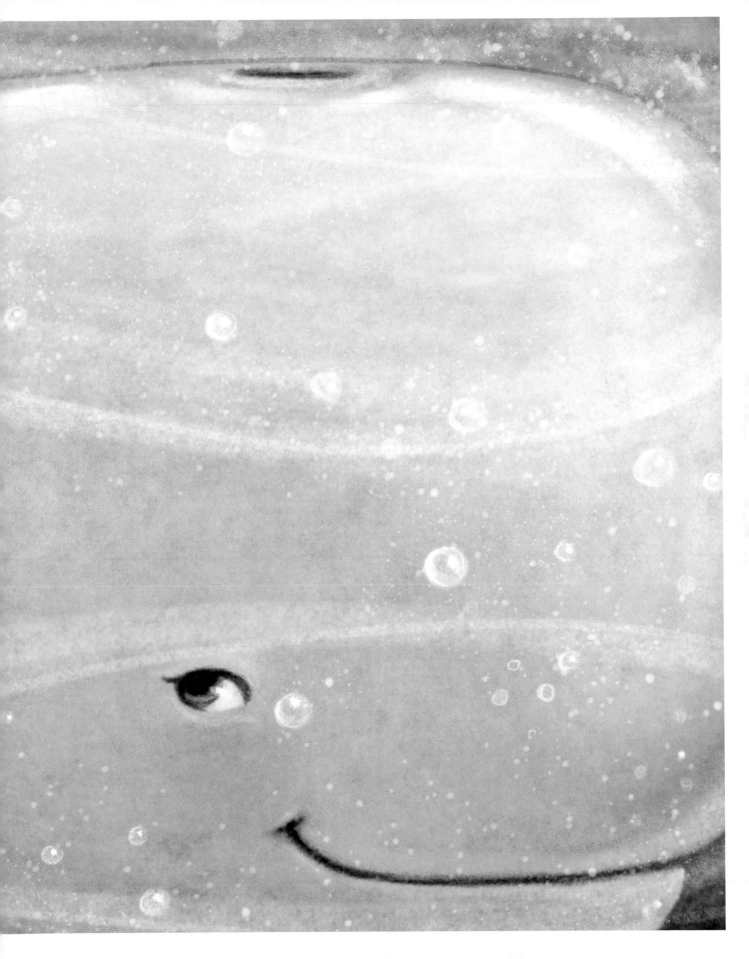

As many fish as there are in the sea,
There's none I'd rather be than me!

Visualize a planet
Where all creatures are one,
And happiness will flower
Brighter than the sun.

A flower is simple, its message is true:

The earth is happy, there are people like you!

Talk a little, sing a lot.
Walk a little, dance a lot.
Smile a little, laugh a lot.
Dream a little, live a lot.

WARNING!
Thoughts become things...
Choose the good ones!

Be free, live now.
Give hope, show how.
Share love, take care.
Stand tall, play fair.
Know right, from wrong.
Be happy, live long.

The call of a whale
To those out of reach,
Echoes a secret
They long to teach:
That material things
Quickly sink out of view,
But time shared with a friend
Is forever with you.

An infinite drop
In an infinite sea,
Like an infinite you
And an infinite me.

Your dreams are gifts
That set you in motion,
On the tides of time
Where life is an ocean.

And your sails are filled
With winds of desire,
To surge through the waves
Of murk and mire.

But when you awaken
With your goal at hand,
You'll see your true destination
Was the voyage not the land.

If all of the people
In all of the world,
Could turn their worries
Into laughter,
Then all of the people
In all of the world,
Would live happily ever after.